There was a rush upon the opening day. The shop was crammed with customers, and there were crowds of mice upon the biscuit canisters.

Sally Henny Penny gets rather flustered when she tries to count out change, and she insists on being paid cash; but she is quite harmless.

And she has laid in a remarkable assortment of bargains. There is something to please everybody.

THE END

Besides—the candles which they sell behave very strangely in warm weather.

And Miss Dormouse refused to take back the ends when they were brought back to her with complaints.

And when Mr. John Dormouse was complained to, he stayed in bed, and would say nothing but "very snug"; which is not the way to carry on a retail business.

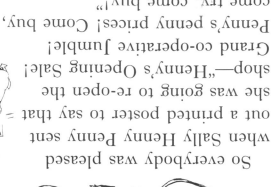

So everybody was pleased when Sally Henny Penny sent out a printed poster to say that she was going to re-open the shop—"Henny's Opening Sale! Grand co-operative Jumble! Penny's penny prices! Come buy, come try, come buy!"

The poster really was most 'ticing.

TOM KITTEN ™ TALES

BEATRIX POTTER

Tom Kitten was quite unable to jump when walking upon his hind legs in trousers. He came up the rockery by degrees, breaking the ferns, and shedding buttons right and left.

TOM KITTEN ™
TALES

THE ORIGINAL AND AUTHORIZED EDITION BY

BEATRIX POTTER

New colour reproductions

FREDERICK WARNE

The reproductions in this book have been made using the most modern electronic scanning methods from entirely new transparencies of Beatrix Potter's original watercolours. They enable Beatrix Potter's skill as an artist to be appreciated as never before, not even during her own lifetime.

FREDERICK WARNE
Published by the Penguin Group
Penguin Books Ltd, 27 Wrights Lane, London W8 5TZ, England
Penguin Putnam Inc., 375 Hudson Street, New York, NY 10014, USA
Penguin Books Australia Ltd, Ringwood, Victoria, Australia
Penguin Books Canada Ltd, 10 Alcorn Avenue, Toronto, Ontario, Canada M4V 3B2
Penguin Books (N.Z.) Ltd, 182-190 Wairau Road, Auckland 10, New Zealand

Penguin Books Ltd, Registered Offices: Harmondsworth, Middlesex, England

First published in 1998 by Frederick Warne

1 3 5 7 9 10 8 6 4 2

ISBN 0 7232 4499 5

Printed and bound in Great Britain by William Clowes Limited, Beccles and London

CONTENTS

BEATRIX POTTER AND HILL TOP FARM

Beatrix (far right) was often photographed by her father. This picture, taken at Dalguise House, is entitled 'After the salmon fishing'.

Beatrix Potter was born in 1866 to Rupert Potter, a well-to-do lawyer, and Helen, the daughter of a wealthy cotton merchant. Beatrix was educated at her London home by governesses and had a rather sheltered Victorian childhood. Each summer, the Potter family rented Dalguise House, a large mansion in Perthshire, Scotland, where their friends and family would gather to go fishing and shooting. Beatrix relished these extended holidays in the countryside, when she and her brother could escape the constraints of London and run wild, exploring the woods and river on the estate. The plants and animals of the Scottish countryside inspired a life-long love of nature in Beatrix.

In 1882, Dalguise House was sold and the Potters adopted the Lake District as their new holiday destination. From her first Lake District holiday, Beatrix was enchanted by the beautiful area. She wrote with regret upon her departure from the picturesque village of Near Sawrey in 1896, 'I was very sorry to come away in spite of the broken weather. It is as nearly perfect a little place as I ever lived in, and such nice old-fashioned people in the village.' So charmed was she by this Lake District village that Beatrix determined to make it her home one day. Using the royalties from her first three books and a small legacy from an aunt, Beatrix purchased Hill Top Farm in Sawrey in 1905. Although she remained dutiful to her elderly parents in London, Beatrix looked forward to her regular trips to Hill Top. Under the management of John Cannon, Hill Top Farm acquired a new wing, a renovated dairy and livestock including ten cows, 14 pigs, ducks, hens and a flock of sheep.

Drawing inspiration from the natural beauty of her surroundings, Beatrix was most productive as an author and artist over the next few years. When her fiancé died suddenly in 1905, Beatrix threw herself into her work and farm to help alleviate her grief. Beatrix's Lake District home provided her with material for the five stories included in this volume, all of which are set in and around Hill Top Farm and the village of Sawrey. She wrote about her new property, 'It is indeed a funny old house and it would amuse children very much.'

Beatrix Potter on Hill Top porch, 1913

Published in 1907, *The Tale of Tom Kitten* is about three misbehaved kittens who spoil their mother's dignified tea party. Any child who has ever been dressed in uncomfortable formal clothes will revel in Tom's mischief! *The Tale of Tom Kitten* is clearly set in Hill Top farmhouse and garden. Mrs. Tabitha Twitchit leads the disobedient kittens indoors through Hill Top's wicket gate, along the pretty garden path and up the house's staircase. Visitors standing on the porch, just as Mrs. Tabitha Twitchit does in the little book, can see the same view across rolling green fields. Beatrix Potter started work on the story in the summer of 1906, while she was in the middle of planning a traditional, unkempt garden at Hill Top. Because the garden at Hill Top has been so carefully preserved, many of the garden scenes in the book can still be identified there today.

Despite the strong association of the Twitchit

The staircase at Hill Top featured in The Tale of Tom Kitten.

Beatrix used the same model for The Tale of Tom Kitten and The Story of Miss Moppet.

Beatrix Potter with her favourite sheepdog, a collie named Kep

family with Hill Top, when Beatrix began sketching *The Tale of Tom Kitten* she did not have a pet cat, and had to borrow one. The kitten proved to be a difficult model—adventurous and mischievous—rather like Tom Kitten himself. On 18th July 1906, she wrote, '. . . I have borrowed a kitten and I am rather glad of the opportunity of working at the drawings. It is very young and pretty and a most fearful pickle.' Although she found the kitten an exasperating model, Beatrix dedicated the Tale to 'all Pickles—especially to those that get upon my garden wall'. Beatrix found ducks easier models than lively kittens. The clothes shed by the kittens in *The Tale of Tom Kitten* are discovered by the Puddle-duck family, who dress themselves in the discarded pinafores and tuckers. While visiting a cousin in London, Beatrix sketched the ducks in Putney Park. Jemima Puddle-duck, a determined but naive character, was the central character in Beatrix's next book, published in 1908.

Set in Hill Top farmyard, *The Tale of Jemima Puddle-Duck* was based on real life events. Jemima was one of the farm ducks who was always wandering off to lay her eggs. The tenant farmer's wife, Mrs. Cannon, had to sometimes substitute a hen to sit on Jemima's neglected eggs. The Cannon family actually appears in the book: we see Mrs. Cannon feeding the poultry, and in another picture her son Ralph looks for eggs among the rhubarb while her daughter, Betsy, passes beyond the gate. This blend of fantasy and reality lends a ring of truth to Beatrix's imaginary world.

Many of Beatrix's real-life animals feature in the Tale. Kep, who rescues Jemima from the fox, was Beatrix's devoted and loyal working sheepdog. Beatrix's Herdwick sheep, a breed native to the Lake District, can be seen in the background, as well as the farm's chickens, horses and cows.

Beatrix enjoyed sketching her farmyard animals, such as these ducks and hen, and closely observed their behaviour.

Observing her farm animals clearly gave Beatrix a lot of pleasure, and she often wrote about them with great affection. 'I seem to be able to tame any sort of animal,' she wrote in a letter, 'it is sometimes rather awkward on a farm, we cannot keep them out of the house, especially the Puddleducks, and turkeys.'

The Tale of Jemima Puddle-Duck is so closely associated with Hill Top Farm that it has been described as 'a poem about the farm itself'. The pictures in the story closely resemble views of Hill Top and the idyllic landscapes surrounding the farm are still recognisable today. The background view, in which Jemima sets off to look for a secret nesting place, can be seen from the far end of the farmyard. The ornamental ironwork gate which leads into a small vegetable garden still exists. In the little village of Near Sawrey, the entrance to the Tower Bank Arms looks very much as it did when Beatrix painted it.

When she bought Hill Top Farm Beatrix Potter decided not to alter the insides at all, and made no modern additions that might change the tone of it. She used it as her studio and study, keeping her

Visitors in Near Sawrey can still have a drink at the Tower Bank Arms.

precious drawings there. One problem facing Beatrix when she moved to Hill Top was an infestation of rats. In a letter to a friend she wrote, 'It really is delightful—if the rats could be stopped out!' Her battle to exterminate the farmhouse rodents, which could be heard overhead scuttering under the floorboards, inspired a story written in 1906. Beatrix always maintained a sense of humour about the rats and dedicated the new book to an intelligent pet rat named Sammy that she had once kept as a pet.

The Tale of Samuel Whiskers continues the adventures of the irrepressible Tom Kitten. Tom climbs up the chimney to hide from his mother and falls into the clutches of an enormous rat named Samuel Whiskers and his subservient wife, Anna Maria. After binding poor Tom, the rats attempt to bake him into a dumpling roly-poly pudding. Fortunately, their plan is thwarted by Tabitha Twitchit and Cousin Ribby, who rescue the errant kitten just in time. Originally called *The Roly-Poly Pudding*, the Tale was first published in 1908 in a large format which allowed Beatrix to include black and white drawings. The story is set in the Twitchit family residence, and thus the illustrations depict the farmhouse: the old-fashioned kitchen range that Tom climbs up, the staircase descended by a frantic Tabitha Twitchit, the dresser that Anna Maria scurries past and the front door through which Cousin Ribby appears are all detailed studies of Hill Top's interior. The scenic landscape seen from the chimney top is a view of Near Sawrey from Hill Top's roof. Beatrix even painted herself

Beatrix used her pet rat, Samuel Whiskers, as her model for this early fantasy picture.

in the story, watching the rats running away from the farmhouse with their wheelbarrow of pilfered goods.

Cousin Ribby is the heroine of the fourth Tale in this collection. Published in 1905, *The Tale of The Pie and The Patty-Pan* was the first story Beatrix set in Near Sawrey and is the only book to mention

A background sketch of the larder at Lakefield Cottage, drawn in 1902

the village by name. When she hears that Cousin Ribby has invited Duchess to tea, an indignant Tabitha Twitchit exclaims, 'A little *dog* indeed! Just as if there were no CATS in Sawrey!' The tea party results in a series of very amusing misunderstandings stemming from the veal and ham pie which Duchess substitutes for Ribby's mouse pie.

Hill Top Farm today

The character of Duchess was based on two Pomeranian dogs belonging to Mrs. Rogerson, the wife of the gardener at Lakefield Cottages. On her third holiday in Sawrey in 1902, Beatrix stayed at Lakefield Cottage and sketched the interior, which became the background for Ribby's home. Duchess

This background painting of Buckle Yeat garden is nearly identical to the illustration in The Tale of The Pie and The Patty-Pan.

A preliminary watercolour of the 'Ginger and Pickles' shop interior

lives at Buckle Yeat, which was then the Near Sawrey Post Office, and the illustration where Duchess reads the invitation shows the Buckle Yeat garden overspilling with poppies and snapdragons. The frontispiece illustration features Hill Top in the background as Ribby crosses the meadow carrying butter and milk.

Duchess lives opposite the village shop that provided the setting for a story published in 1909. *The Tale of Ginger and Pickles* is about a tom-cat and terrier who run a village store. To the dismay of their customers, they are bankrupted by giving unlimited credit and close the shop. Dedicated to the owner of the village shop in Near Sawrey, the story proved popular with the villagers and Beatrix described their reaction in a letter to a friend. 'The "Ginger & Pickle" book has been causing much amusement, it has got a good many views which can be recognised in the village which is what they like, they are all quite jealous of each others houses & cats getting into a book.'

Originally published in a large format, the bigger size enabled Beatrix to depict the shop interior in detail. The story features familiar friends from previous books. Tom Kitten, Mittens and Moppet peer through the shop window in the frontispiece. Samuel Whiskers, who has run up a long bill for bacon and snuff, waits at the counter. The shopkeepers suspect Anna Maria of stealing cream crackers and Jemima Puddle-duck is pictured shopping with her ducklings. *The Tale of Ginger and Pickles,* a celebration of Sawrey, unites both Beatrix's fictional and real-life village.

In 1909 Beatrix purchased Castle Farm, with fields adjoining Hill Top. Visitors to the Lake District admire its rolling landscapes and traditional farmhouses, but the area famous for its unspoilt beauty might look very different today but for Beatrix Potter's foresight. She felt a great need to keep her beloved Lake District preserved for future generations, and dedicated the last 30 years of her life to ensuring that the area remained untouched by developers. A practical businesswoman, Beatrix efficiently managed some estates for the National Trust. When she died in 1943, Beatrix Potter left 4,000 acres of land to the nation. She dearly loved the countryside, and in her seventies she wrote, '. . . as I lie in bed, I can walk step by step on the fells and rough lands, seeing every stone and flower . . . where my old legs will never take me again.' It is a measure of the strength of her convictions and her extraordinary character that she was able to make her dreams a reality.

Troutbeck Park Farm, purchased in 1924, was one of the many farms that Beatrix bequeathed to the National Trust.

Beatrix won many prizes for her Herdwick ewes and often judged sheep at local agricultural shows.

The Tale of Tom Kitten

1907

ONCE upon a time there were three little kittens, and their names were Mittens, Tom Kitten, and Moppet.

They had dear little fur coats of their own; and they tumbled about the doorstep and played in the dust.

But one day their mother—Mrs. Tabitha Twitchit—expected friends to tea; so she fetched the kittens indoors, to wash and dress them, before the fine company arrived.

First she scrubbed their faces (this one is Moppet).

Then she brushed their fur (this one is Mittens).

Then she combed their tails and whiskers (this is Tom Kitten).

Tom was very naughty, and he scratched.

Mrs. Tabitha dressed Moppet and Mittens in clean pinafores and tuckers; and then she took all sorts of elegant uncomfortable clothes out of a chest of drawers, in order to dress up her son Thomas.

Tom Kitten was very fat, and he had grown; several buttons burst off. His mother sewed them on again.

When the three kittens were ready, Mrs. Tabitha unwisely turned them out into the garden, to be out of the way while she made hot buttered toast.

"Now keep your frocks clean, children! You must walk on your hind legs. Keep away from the dirty ash-pit, and from Sally Henny Penny, and from the pig-stye and the Puddle-ducks."

Moppet and Mittens walked down the garden path unsteadily. Presently they trod upon their pinafores and fell on their noses. When they stood up there were several green smears!

"Let us climb up the rockery, and sit on the garden wall," said Moppet.

They turned their pinafores back to front, and went up with a skip and a jump; Moppet's white tucker fell down into the road.

Tom Kitten was quite unable to jump when walking upon his hind legs in trousers. He came up the rockery by degrees, breaking the ferns, and shedding buttons right and left.

He was all in pieces when he reached the top of the wall.

Moppet and Mittens tried to pull him together; his hat fell off, and the rest of his buttons burst.

While they were in difficulties, there was a pit pat paddle pat! and the three Puddle-ducks came along the hard high road, marching one behind the other and doing the goose step— pit pat paddle pat! Pit pat waddle pat!

They stopped and stood in a row, and stared up at the kittens. They had very small eyes and looked surprised.

Then the two duck-birds, Rebeccah and Jemima Puddle-duck, picked up the hat and tucker and put them on.

Mittens laughed so that she fell off the wall. Moppet and Tom descended after her; the pinafores and all the rest of Tom's clothes came off on the way down.

"Come! Mr. Drake Puddle-duck," said Moppet—"Come and help us to dress him! Come and button up Tom!"

Mr. Drake Puddle-duck advanced in a slow sideways manner, and picked up the various articles.

But he put them on *himself!* They fitted him even worse than Tom Kitten.

"It's a very fine morning!" said Mr. Drake Puddle-duck.

And he and Jemima and Rebeccah Puddle-duck set off up the road, keeping step— pit pat, paddle pat! Pit pat, waddle pat!

Then Tabitha Twitchit came down the garden and found her kittens on the wall with no clothes on.

She pulled them off the wall, smacked them, and took them back to the house.

"My friends will arrive in a minute, and you are not fit to be seen; I am affronted," said Mrs. Tabitha Twitchit.

She sent them upstairs; and I am sorry to say she told her friends that they were in bed with the measles; which was not true.

Quite the contrary; they were not in bed: *not* in the least.

Somehow there were very extraordinary noises over-head, which disturbed the dignity and repose of the tea party.

And I think that some day I shall have to make another, larger, book, to tell you more about Tom Kitten!

As for the Puddle-ducks— they went into a pond.

The clothes all came off directly, because there were no buttons.

And Mr. Drake Puddle-duck, and Jemima and Rebeccah, have been looking for them ever since.

THE END

The Tale of Jemima Puddle-Duck

1908

WHAT a funny sight it is to see a brood of ducklings with a hen!

—Listen to the story of Jemima Puddle-duck, who was annoyed because the farmer's wife would not let her hatch her own eggs.

Her sister-in-law, Mrs. Rebeccah Puddle-duck, was perfectly willing to leave the hatching to someone else—

"I have not the patience to sit on a nest for twenty-eight days; and no more have you, Jemima. You would let them go cold; you know you would!"

"I wish to hatch my own eggs; I will hatch them all by myself," quacked Jemima Puddle-duck.

She tried to hide her eggs; but they were always found and carried off.

Jemima Puddle-duck became quite desperate. She determined to make a nest right away from the farm.

She set off on a fine spring afternoon along the cart-road that leads over the hill.

She was wearing a shawl and a poke bonnet.

When she reached the top of the hill, she saw a wood in the distance.

She thought that it looked a safe quiet spot.

Jemima Puddle-duck was not much in the habit of flying. She ran downhill a few yards flapping her shawl, and then she jumped off into the air.

She flew beautifully when she had got a good start.

She skimmed along over the tree-tops until she saw an open place in the middle of the wood, where the trees and brushwood had been cleared.

Jemima alighted rather heavily, and began to waddle about in search of a convenient dry nesting-place.

She rather fancied a tree-stump amongst some tall fox-gloves.

But—seated upon the stump, she was startled to find an elegantly dressed gentleman reading a newspaper.

He had black prick ears and sandy-coloured whiskers.

"Quack?" said Jemima Puddle-duck, with her head and her bonnet on one side— "Quack?"

The gentleman raised his eyes above his newspaper and looked curiously at Jemima—

"Madam, have you lost your way?" said he. He had a long bushy tail which he was sitting upon, as the stump was somewhat damp.

Jemima thought him mighty civil and handsome. She explained that she had not lost her way, but that she was trying to find a convenient dry nesting-place.

"Ah! Is that so? Indeed!" said the gentleman with sandy whiskers, looking curiously at Jemima. He folded up the newspaper, and put it in his coat-tail pocket.

Jemima complained of the superfluous hen.

"Indeed! How interesting!

I wish I could meet with that fowl. I would teach it to mind its own business!

"But as to a nest—there is no difficulty: I have a sackful of feathers in my woodshed. No, my dear madam, you will be in nobody's way. You may sit there as long as you like," said the bushy long-tailed gentleman.

He led the way to a very retired, dismal-looking house amongst the fox-gloves.

It was built of faggots and turf, and there were two broken pails, one on top of another, by way of a chimney.

"This is my summer residence; you would not find my earth—my winter house— so convenient," said the hospitable gentleman.

There was a tumble-down shed at the back of the house, made of old soap-boxes. The gentleman opened the door, and showed Jemima in.

The shed was almost quite full of feathers—it was almost suffocating; but it was comfortable and very soft.

Jemima Puddle-duck was rather surprised to find such a vast quantity of feathers. But it was very comfortable; and she made a nest without any trouble at all.

When she came out, the sandy-whiskered gentleman was sitting on a log reading the newspaper—at least he had it spread out, but he was looking over the top of it.

He was so polite, that he seemed almost sorry to let Jemima go home for the night. He promised to take great care of her nest until she came back again next day.

He said he loved eggs and ducklings; he should be proud to see a fine nestful in his wood-shed.

Jemima Puddle-duck came every afternoon; she laid nine eggs in the nest. They were greeny white and very large. The

foxy gentleman admired them immensely. He used to turn them over and count them when Jemima was not there.

At last Jemima told him that she intended to begin to sit next

day—"and I will bring a bag of
corn with me, so that I need
never leave my nest until the
eggs are hatched. They might
catch cold," said the
conscientious Jemima.

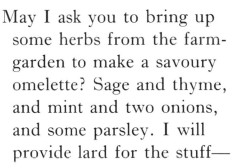

"Madam, I beg you not to
trouble yourself with a bag; I
will provide oats. But before you
commence your tedious sitting,
I intend to give you a treat. Let us
have a dinner-party all to ourselves! May I ask you to bring up
some herbs from the farm-
garden to make a savoury
omelette? Sage and thyme,
and mint and two onions,
and some parsley. I will
provide lard for the stuff—

lard for the omelette," said the
hospitable gentleman with sandy
whiskers.

Jemima Puddle-duck was a
simpleton: not even the mention of
sage and onions made her suspicious.

She went round the farm-garden, nibbling off snippets of all
the different sorts of herbs that are used for stuffing roast duck.

And she waddled into the kitchen, and got two onions out of a basket.

The collie-dog Kep met her coming out. "What are you doing with those onions? Where do you go every afternoon by yourself, Jemima Puddle-duck?"

Jemima was rather in awe of the collie; she told him the whole story.

The collie listened, with his wise head on one side; he grinned when she described the polite gentleman with sandy whiskers.

He asked several questions about the wood, and about the exact position of the house and shed.

Then he went out, and trotted down the village. He went to look for two fox-hound puppies who were out at walk with the butcher.

Jemima Puddle-duck went up the cart-road for the last time, on a sunny afternoon. She was rather burdened with bunches of herbs and two onions in a bag.

She flew over the wood, and alighted opposite the house of the bushy long-tailed gentleman.

He was sitting on a log; he sniffed the air, and kept glancing uneasily round the wood. When Jemima alighted he quite jumped.

"Come into the house as soon as you have looked at your eggs. Give me the herbs for the omelette. Be sharp!"

He was rather abrupt. Jemima Puddle-duck had never heard him speak like that.

She felt surprised, and uncomfortable.

While she was inside she heard pattering feet round the back of the shed. Some-one with a black nose sniffed at the bottom of the door, and then locked it.

Jemima became much alarmed.

A moment afterwards there were most awful noises—barking, baying, growls and howls, squealing and groans.

And nothing more was ever seen of that foxy-whiskered gentleman.

Presently Kep opened the door of the shed, and let out Jemima Puddle-duck.

Unfortunately the puppies rushed in and gobbled up all the eggs before he could stop them.

He had a bite on his ear and both the puppies were limping.
Jemima Puddle-duck was escorted home in tears on account
of those eggs.

She laid some more in June, and she was permitted to keep them herself: but only four of them hatched.

Jemima Puddle-duck said that it was because of her nerves; but she had always been a bad sitter.

THE END

THE TALE OF
SAMUEL WHISKERS
OR
THE ROLY-POLY PUDDING

1908

ONCE upon a time there was an old cat, called Mrs. Tabitha Twitchit, who was an anxious parent. She used to lose her kittens continually, and whenever they were lost they were always in mischief!

On baking day she determined to shut them up in a cupboard.

She caught Moppet and Mittens, but she could not find Tom.

Mrs. Tabitha went up and down all over the house, mewing for Tom Kitten. She looked in the pantry under the staircase, and she searched the best spare bedroom that was all covered up with dust sheets. She went right upstairs and looked into the attics, but she could not find him anywhere.

It was an old, old house, full of cupboards and passages. Some of the walls were four feet thick, and there used to be queer noises inside them, as if there might be a little secret staircase. Certainly there were odd little jagged doorways in the wainscot, and things disappeared at night—especially cheese and bacon.

Mrs. Tabitha became more and more distracted, and mewed dreadfully.

While their mother was searching the house, Moppet and Mittens had got into mischief.

The cupboard door was not locked, so they pushed it open and came out.

They went straight to the
dough which was set to rise
in a pan before the fire.

They patted it with their
little soft paws—"Shall we
make dear little muffins?"
said Mittens to Moppet.

But just at that moment
somebody knocked at the
front door, and Moppet
jumped into the flour barrel
in a fright.

Mittens ran away to the
dairy, and hid in an empty
jar on the stone shelf where
the milk pans stand.

The visitor was a neighbour,
Mrs. Ribby; she had called to
borrow some yeast.

Mrs. Tabitha came downstairs mewing dreadfully—"Come
in, Cousin Ribby, come in, and sit ye down! I'm in sad
trouble, Cousin Ribby," said Tabitha, shedding tears. "I've lost
my dear son Thomas; I'm afraid the rats have got him." She
wiped her eyes with her apron.

"He's a bad kitten, Cousin Tabitha; he made a cat's cradle of
my best bonnet last time I came to tea. Where have you looked
for him?"

"All over the house! The
rats are too many for me.
What a thing it is to have an
unruly family!" said Mrs.
Tabitha Twitchit.

"I'm not afraid of rats;
I will help you to find him;
and whip him too! What is
all that soot in the fender?"

"The chimney wants
sweeping—Oh, dear me,
Cousin Ribby—now Moppet
and Mittens are gone!

"They have both got out of
the cupboard!"

Ribby and Tabitha set to
work to search the house
thoroughly again. They poked
under the beds with Ribby's umbrella, and they rummaged in
cupboards. They even fetched a candle, and looked inside a

clothes chest in one of
the attics. They could
not find anything, but
once they heard a door
bang and somebody
scuttered downstairs.

"Yes, it is infested
with rats," said Tabitha
tearfully. "I caught
seven young ones out
of one hole in the back
kitchen, and we had
them for dinner last
Saturday. And once I
saw the old father rat
—an enormous old rat,
Cousin Ribby. I was
just going to jump
upon him, when he

showed his yellow teeth at me and whisked down the hole.

"The rats get upon my nerves, Cousin Ribby," said Tabitha.

Ribby and Tabitha searched and searched. They both heard a curious roly-poly noise under the attic floor. But there was nothing to be seen.

They returned to the kitchen. "Here's one of your kittens at least," said Ribby, dragging Moppet out of the flour barrel.

They shook the flour off her and set her down on the kitchen floor. She seemed to be in a terrible fright.

"Oh! Mother, Mother," said Moppet, "there's been an old woman rat in the kitchen, and she's stolen some of the dough!"

The two cats ran to look at the dough pan. Sure enough there were marks of little scratching fingers, and a lump of dough was gone!

"Which way did she go, Moppet?"

But Moppet had been too much frightened to peep out of the barrel again.

Ribby and Tabitha took her with them to keep her safely in sight, while they went on with their search.

They went into the dairy.

The first thing they found was Mittens, hiding in an empty jar.

They tipped up the jar, and she scrambled out.

"Oh, Mother, Mother!" said Mittens—

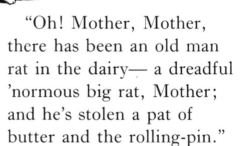

"Oh! Mother, Mother, there has been an old man rat in the dairy— a dreadful 'normous big rat, Mother; and he's stolen a pat of butter and the rolling-pin."

Ribby and Tabitha looked at one another.

"A rolling-pin and butter! Oh, my poor son Thomas!" exclaimed Tabitha, wringing her paws.

"A rolling-pin?" said Ribby. "Did we not hear a roly-poly noise in the attic when we were looking into that chest?"

Ribby and Tabitha rushed upstairs again. Sure enough the roly-poly noise was still going on quite distinctly under the attic floor.

"This is serious, Cousin
Tabitha," said Ribby. "We
must send for John Joiner
at once, with a saw."

*   *   *   *   *

Now this is what had been happening to Tom Kitten, and it
shows how very unwise it is to go up a chimney in a very old
house, where a person does not know his way, and where there
are enormous rats.

Tom Kitten did not want
to be shut up in a cupboard.
When he saw that his
mother was going to bake,
he determined to hide.

He looked about for a nice
convenient place, and he
fixed upon the chimney.

The fire had only just been lighted, and it was not hot; but
there was a white choky smoke from the green sticks. Tom
Kitten got upon the fender and looked up. It was a big
old-fashioned fire-place.

The chimney itself was wide enough inside for a man to
stand up and walk about. So there was plenty of room for a
little Tom Cat.

He jumped right up into the fire-place, balancing himself
upon the iron bar where the kettle hangs.

Tom Kitten took another big jump off the bar, and landed on a ledge high up inside the chimney, knocking down some soot into the fender.

Tom Kitten coughed and choked with the smoke; and he could hear the sticks beginning to crackle and burn in the fire-place down below. He made up his mind to climb right to the top, and get out on the slates, and try to catch sparrows.

"I cannot go back. If I slipped I might fall in the fire and singe my beautiful tail and my little blue jacket."

The chimney was a very big old-fashioned one. It was built in the days when people burnt logs of wood upon the hearth.

The chimney stack stood up above the roof like a little stone tower, and the daylight shone down from the top, under the slanting slates that kept out the rain.

Tom Kitten was getting very frightened! He climbed up, and up, and up.

Then he waded sideways through inches of soot. He was like a little sweep himself.

It was most confusing in the dark. One flue seemed to lead into another.

There was less smoke, but Tom Kitten felt quite lost.

He scrambled up and up; but before he reached the chimney top he came to a place where somebody had loosened a stone in the wall. There were some mutton bones lying about—

"This seems funny," said Tom Kitten. "Who has been gnawing bones up here in the chimney? I wish I had never come! And what a funny smell? It is something like mouse; only dreadfully strong. It makes me sneeze," said Tom Kitten.

He squeezed through the hole in the wall, and dragged himself along a most uncomfortably tight passage where there was scarcely any light.

He groped his way carefully for several yards; he was at the back of the skirting-board in the attic, where there is a little mark * in the picture.

All at once he fell head over heels in the dark, down a hole, and landed on a heap of very dirty rags.

When Tom Kitten picked himself up and looked about him—he found himself in a place that he had never seen before,

although he had lived all his life in the house.

It was a very small stuffy fusty room, with boards, and rafters, and cobwebs, and lath and plaster.

Opposite to him—as far away as he could sit—was an enormous rat.

"What do you mean by tumbling into my

bed all covered with smuts?" said the rat, chattering his teeth.

"Please sir, the chimney wants sweeping," said poor Tom Kitten.

"Anna Maria! Anna Maria!" squeaked the rat. There was a pattering noise and an old woman rat poked her head round a rafter.

All in a minute she rushed upon Tom Kitten, and before he knew what was happening—

His coat was pulled off, and he was rolled up in a bundle, and tied with string in very hard knots.

Anna Maria did the tying. The old rat watched her and took snuff. When she had finished, they both sat staring at him with their mouths open.

"Anna Maria," said the old man rat (whose name was Samuel Whiskers), "Anna Maria, make me a kitten dumpling roly-poly pudding for my dinner."

"It requires dough and a pat of butter, and a rolling-pin,' said Anna Maria, considering Tom Kitten with her head on one side.

"No," said Samuel Whiskers, "make it properly, Anna Maria, with breadcrumbs."

"Nonsense! Butter and dough," replied Anna Maria.

The two rats consulted together for a few minutes and then went away.

Samuel Whiskers got through a hole in the wainscot, and went boldly down the front staircase to the dairy to get the butter. He did not meet anybody.

He made a second journey for the rolling-pin. He pushed it in front of him with his paws, like a brewer's man trundling a barrel.

He could hear Ribby and Tabitha talking, but they were busy lighting the candle to look into the chest. They did not see him.

Anna Maria went down by way of the skirting-board and a window shutter to the kitchen to steal the dough.

She borrowed a small saucer, and scooped up the dough with her paws.

She did not observe Moppet.

While Tom Kitten was left alone under the floor of the attic, he wriggled about and tried to mew for help.

But his mouth was full of soot and cobwebs, and he was tied up in such very tight knots, he could not make anybody hear him.

Except a spider, which came out of a crack in the ceiling and

examined the knots critically, from a safe distance.

It was a judge of knots because it had a habit of tying up unfortunate bluc-bottles. It did not offer to assist him.

Tom Kitten wriggled and squirmed until he was quite exhausted.

Presently the rats came back and set to work to make him into a dumpling. First they smeared him with butter, and then they rolled him in the dough.

"Will not the string be very indigestible, Anna Maria?" inquired Samuel Whiskers.

Anna Maria said she thought that it was of no consequence; but she wished that Tom Kitten would hold his head still, as it disarranged the pastry.
She laid hold of his ears.

Tom Kitten bit and spat, and mewed and wriggled; and the rolling-pin went roly-poly, roly; roly, poly, roly. The rats each held an end.

"His tail is sticking out! You did not fetch enough dough, Anna Maria."

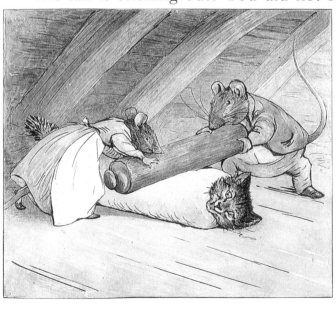

"I fetched as much as I could carry," replied Anna Maria.

"I do not think"— said Samuel Whiskers, pausing to take a look at Tom Kitten—"I do *not* think it will be a good pudding. It smells sooty."

Anna Maria was about to argue the

point, when all at once there began to be other sounds up above—the rasping noise of a saw; and the noise of a little dog, scratching and yelping!

The rats dropped the rolling-pin, and listened attentively.

"We are discovered and interrupted, Anna Maria; let us collect our property—and other people's,—and depart at once."

"I fear that we shall be obliged to leave this pudding."

"But I am persuaded that the knots would have proved indigestible, whatever you may urge to the contrary."

"Come away at once and help me to tie up some mutton bones in a counterpane," said Anna Maria. "I have got half a smoked ham hidden in the chimney."

So it happened that by the time John Joiner had got the plank up—there was nobody under the floor except the rolling-pin and Tom Kitten in a very dirty dumpling!

But there was a strong smell of rats; and John Joiner spent the rest of the morning sniffing and whining, and wagging his tail, and going round and round with his head in the hole like a gimlet.

Then he nailed the plank down again and put his tools in his bag, and came downstairs.

The cat family had quite recovered. They invited him to stay to dinner.

The dumpling had been peeled off Tom Kitten, and made separately into a bag pudding, with currants in it to hide the smuts.

They had been obliged to put Tom Kitten into a hot bath to get the butter off.

John Joiner smelt the pudding; but he regretted that he had not time to stay to dinner, because he had just finished making a wheel-barrow for Miss Potter, and she had ordered two hen-coops.

And when I was going to the post late in the afternoon—I looked up the lane from the corner, and I saw Mr. Samuel Whiskers and his wife on the run, with big bundles on a little wheel-barrow, which looked very like mine.

They were just turning in at the gate to the barn of Farmer Potatoes.

Samuel Whiskers was puffing and out of breath. Anna Maria was still arguing in shrill tones.

She seemed to know her way, and she seemed to have a quantity of luggage.

I am sure *I* never gave her leave to borrow my wheel-barrow!

They went into the barn, and hauled their parcels with a bit of string to the top of the hay mow.

After that, there were no more rats for a long time at Tabitha Twitchit's.

As for Farmer Potatoes, he has been driven nearly distracted. There are rats, and rats, and rats in his barn! They eat up the chicken food, and steal the oats and bran, and make holes in the meal bags.

And they are all descended from Mr. and Mrs. Samuel Whiskers—children and grand-children and great great grand-children.

There is no end to them!

Moppet and Mittens have grown up into very good rat-catchers.

They go out rat-catching in the village, and they find plenty of employment. They charge so much a dozen, and earn their living very comfortably.

They hang up the rats' tails in a row on the barn door, to show how many they have caught—dozens and dozens of them.

But Tom Kitten has always been afraid of a rat; he never durst face anything that is bigger than—

A Mouse.

THE END

THE TALE OF
THE PIE
AND THE PATTY-PAN

1905

ONCE upon a time there was a Pussy-cat called Ribby, who invited a little dog called Duchess, to tea.

"Come in good time, my dear Duchess," said Ribby's letter, "and we will have something so very nice. I am baking it in a pie-dish—a pie-dish with a pink rim. You never tasted anything so good! And *you* shall eat it all! *I* will eat muffins, my dear Duchess!" wrote Ribby.

Duchess read the letter and wrote an answer:—"I will come with much pleasure at a quarter past four. But it is very strange. *I* was just going to invite you to come here, to supper, my dear Ribby, to eat something *most delicious.*

"I will come very punctually, my dear Ribby," wrote Duchess; and then at the end she added—"I hope it isn't mouse?"

And then she thought that did not look quite polite; so she scratched out "isn't mouse" and changed it to "I hope it will be fine," and she gave her letter to the postman.

But she thought a great deal about Ribby's pie, and she read Ribby's letter over and over again.

"I am dreadfully afraid it *will* be mouse!" said Duchess to herself—"I really couldn't, *couldn't* eat mouse pie. And I shall have to eat it, because it is a party. And *my* pie was going to be veal and ham. A pink and white pie-dish! and so is mine; just like Ribby's dishes; they were both bought at Tabitha Twitchit's."

Duchess went into her
larder and took the pie off
a shelf and looked at it.

"It is all ready to put into
the oven. Such lovely
pie-crust; and I put in a
little tin patty-pan to hold
up the crust; and I made a
hole in the middle with a
fork to let out the steam—
Oh I do wish I could eat my own pie, instead of a pie made of
mouse!"

Duchess considered and considered and read Ribby's letter
again—

"A pink and white pie-dish—and *you* shall eat it *all*. 'You'
means me—then Ribby is not going to even taste the pie herself?
A pink and white pie-dish! Ribby is sure to go out to buy the
muffins . . . Oh what a good idea! Why shouldn't I rush along
and put my pie into Ribby's oven when Ribby isn't there?"

Duchess was quite delighted with her own cleverness!

Ribby in the meantime had received Duchess's answer, and as
soon as she was sure that the little dog could come—she popped

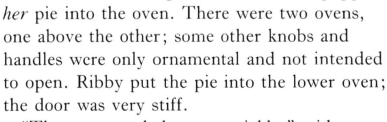

her pie into the oven. There were two ovens,
one above the other; some other knobs and
handles were only ornamental and not intended
to open. Ribby put the pie into the lower oven;
the door was very stiff.

"The top oven bakes too quickly," said
Ribby to herself. "It is a pie of the most
delicate and tender mouse minced up with
bacon. And I have taken out all the bones;

because Duchess did nearly choke herself with a fish-bone last time I gave a party. She eats a little fast—rather big mouthfuls. But a most genteel and elegant little dog; infinitely superior company to Cousin Tabitha Twitchit."

Ribby put on some coal and swept up the hearth. Then she went out with a can to the well, for water to fill up the kettle.

Then she began to set the room in order, for it was the sitting-room as well as the kitchen. She shook the mats out at the front door and put them straight; the hearth-rug was a rabbit-skin. She dusted the clock and the ornaments on the mantelpiece, and she polished and rubbed the tables and chairs.

Then she spread a very clean white table-cloth, and set out her best china tea-set, which she took out of a wall-cupboard near the fireplace.

The tea-cups were white with a pattern of pink roses; and the dinner-plates were white and blue.

When Ribby had laid the table she took a jug and a blue and white dish, and went out down the field to the farm, to fetch milk and butter.

When she came back, she peeped into the bottom oven; the pie looked very comfortable.

Ribby put on her shawl and bonnet and went out again with a basket, to the village

shop to buy a packet of tea, a pound of lump sugar, and a pot of marmalade.

And just at the same time, Duchess came out of *her* house, at the other end of the village.

Ribby met Duchess half-way down the street, also carrying a basket, covered with a cloth. They only bowed to one another;

they did not speak, because they were going to have a party.

As soon as Duchess had got round the corner out of sight—she simply ran! Straight away to Ribby's house!

Ribby went into the shop and bought what she required, and came out, after a pleasant gossip with Cousin Tabitha Twitchit.

Cousin Tabitha was disdainful afterwards in conversation—

"A little *dog* indeed! Just as if there were no CATS in Sawrey! And a *pie* for afternoon tea! The very idea!" said Cousin Tabitha Twitchit.

Ribby went on to Timothy Baker's and bought the muffins. Then she went home.

There seemed to be a sort of scuffling noise in the back passage, as she was coming in at the front door.

"I trust that is not that Pie: the spoons are locked up, however," said Ribby.

But there was nobody there. Ribby opened the bottom oven door with some difficulty, and turned the pie. There began to be a pleasing smell of baked mouse!

Duchess in the meantime, had slipped out at the back door.

"It is a very odd thing that Ribby's pie was *not* in the oven when I put mine in! And I can't find it anywhere; I have looked all over the house. I put *my* pie into a nice hot oven at the top. I could not turn any of the other handles; I think that they are all shams," said Duchess, "but I wish I could have removed the pie made of mouse! I cannot think what she has done with it? I heard Ribby coming and I had to run out by the back door!"

Duchess went home and brushed her beautiful black coat; and then she picked a bunch of flowers in her garden as a present for Ribby; and passed the time until the clock struck four.

Ribby—having assured herself by careful search that there was really no one hiding in the cupboard or in the larder—went upstairs to change her dress.

She put on a lilac silk gown, for the party, and an embroidered muslin apron and tippet.

"It is very strange," said Ribby, "I did not *think* I left that drawer pulled out; has somebody been trying on my mittens?"

She came downstairs again, and made the tea, and put the teapot on the hob. She peeped again into the *bottom* oven, the pie had become a lovely brown, and it was steaming hot.

She sat down before the fire to wait for the little dog. "I am glad I used the *bottom* oven," said Ribby, "the top one would certainly have been very much too hot. I wonder why that cupboard door was open? Can there really have been someone in the house?"

Very punctually at four o'clock, Duchess started to go to the party. She ran so fast through the village that she was too early, and she had to wait a little while in the lane that leads down to Ribby's house.

"I wonder if Ribby has taken *my* pie out of the oven yet?" said Duchess, "and whatever can have become of the other pie made of mouse?"

At a quarter past four to the minute, there came a most genteel little tap-tappity. "Is Mrs. Ribston at home?" inquired Duchess in the porch.

"Come in! and how do you do, my dear Duchess?" cried Ribby. "I hope I see you well?"

"Quite well, I thank you, and how do *you* do, my dear Ribby?" said Duchess. "I've brought you some flowers; what a delicious smell of pie!"

"Oh, what lovely flowers! Yes, it is mouse and bacon!"

"Do not talk about food, my dear Ribby," said Duchess; "what a lovely white tea-cloth! . . . Is it done to a turn? Is it still in the oven?"

"I think it wants another five minutes," said Ribby. "Just a shade longer; I will pour out the tea, while we wait. Do you take sugar, my dear Duchess?"

"Oh yes, please! my dear Ribby; and may I have a lump upon my nose?"

"With pleasure, my dear Duchess; how beautifully you beg! Oh, how sweetly pretty!"

Duchess sat up with the sugar on her nose and sniffed—

"How good that pie smells! I do love veal and ham—I mean to say mouse and bacon—"

She dropped the sugar in confusion, and had to go hunting under the tea-table, so did not see which oven Ribby opened in order to get out the pie.

Ribby set the pie upon the table; there was a very savoury smell.

Duchess came out from under the table-cloth munching sugar, and sat up on a chair.

"I will first cut the pie for you; I am going to have muffin and marmalade," said Ribby.

"Do you really prefer muffin? Mind the patty-pan!"

"I beg your pardon?" said Ribby.

"May I pass you the marmalade?" said Duchess hurriedly.

The pie proved extremely toothsome, and the muffins light and hot. They disappeared rapidly, especially the pie!

"I think"—(thought the Duchess to herself)—"I *think* it would be wiser if I helped myself to pie; though Ribby did not seem to notice anything when she was cutting it. What very small fine pieces it has cooked into! I did not remember that I had minced it up so fine; I suppose this is a quicker oven than my own."

"How fast Duchess is eating!" thought Ribby to herself, as she buttered her fifth muffin.

The pie-dish was emptying rapidly! Duchess had had four helps already, and was fumbling with the spoon.

"A little more bacon, my dear Duchess?" said Ribby.

"Thank you, my dear Ribby; I was only feeling for the patty-pan."

"The patty-pan? my dear Duchess?"

"The patty-pan that held up the pie-crust," said Duchess, blushing under her black coat.

"Oh, I didn't put one in, my dear Duchess," said Ribby; "I don't think that it is necessary in pies made of mouse."

Duchess fumbled with the spoon—"I can't find it!" she said anxiously.

"There isn't a patty-pan," said Ribby, looking perplexed.

"Yes, indeed, my dear Ribby; where can it have gone to?" said Duchess.

"There most certainly is not one, my dear Duchess. I disapprove of tin articles in puddings and pies. It is most

undesirable—(especially when people swallow in lumps!)" she added in a lower voice.

Duchess looked very much alarmed, and continued to scoop the inside of the pie-dish.

"My Great-aunt Squintina (grandmother of Cousin Tabitha Twitchit) —died of a thimble in a Christmas plum-pudding. *I* never put any article of metal in *my* puddings or pies."

Duchess looked aghast, and tilted up the pie-dish.

"I have only four patty-pans, and they are all in the cupboard."

Duchess set up a howl.

"I shall die! I shall die! I have swallowed a patty-pan! Oh, my dear Ribby, I do feel so ill!"

"It is impossible, my dear Duchess; there was not a patty-pan."

Duchess moaned and whined and rocked herself about.

"Oh I feel so dreadful, I have swallowed a patty-pan!"

"There was *nothing* in the pie," said Ribby severely.

"Yes there *was,* my dear Ribby, I am sure I have swallowed it!"

"Let me prop you up with a pillow, my dear Duchess; where do you think you feel it?"

"Oh I do feel so ill *all over* me, my dear Ribby; I have swallowed a large tin patty-pan with a sharp scalloped edge!"

"Shall I run for the doctor? I will just lock up the spoons!"

"Oh yes, yes! fetch Dr. Maggotty, my dear Ribby: he is a Pie himself, he will certainly understand."

Ribby settled Duchess in an armchair before the fire, and went out and hurried to the village to look for the doctor.

She found him at the smithy.

He was occupied in putting rusty nails into a bottle of ink, which he had obtained at the post office.

"Gammon? ha! HA!" said he, with his head on one side.

Ribby explained that her guest had swallowed a patty-pan.

"Spinach? ha! HA!" said he, and accompanied her with alacrity.

He hopped so fast that Ribby had to run. It was most conspicuous. All the village could see that Ribby was fetching the doctor.

"I *knew* that they would over-eat themselves!" said Cousin Tabitha Twitchit.

But while Ribby had been hunting for the doctor—a curious thing had happened to Duchess, who had been left by herself, sitting before the fire, sighing and groaning and feeling very unhappy.

"How *could* I have swallowed it! such a large thing as a patty-pan!"

She got up and went to the table, and felt inside the pie-dish again with a spoon.

"No; there is no patty-pan, and I put one in; and nobody has eaten pie except me, so I must have swallowed it!"

She sat down again, and stared mournfully at the grate. The fire crackled and danced, and something sizz-z-zled!

Duchess started! She opened the door of the *top* oven;—out came a rich steamy flavour of veal and ham, and there stood a fine brown pie,—and through a hole in the top of the pie-crust there was a glimpse of a little tin patty-pan!

Duchess drew a long breath—

"Then I must have been eating MOUSE! . . . No wonder I feel ill . . . But perhaps I should feel worse if I had really swallowed a patty-pan!" Duchess reflected—"What a very awkward thing to have to explain to Ribby! I think I will put *my* pie in the back-yard and say nothing about it. When I go home, I will run round and take it away." She put it outside

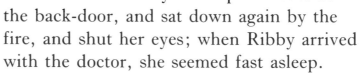

the back-door, and sat down again by the fire, and shut her eyes; when Ribby arrived with the doctor, she seemed fast asleep.

"Gammon, ha, HA?" said the doctor.

"I am feeling very much better," said Duchess, waking up with a jump.

"I am truly glad to hear it! He has brought you a pill, my dear Duchess!"

"I think I should feel *quite* well if he only felt my pulse," said Duchess, backing away from the magpie, who sidled up with something in his beak.

"It is only a bread pill, you had much better take it; drink a little milk, my dear Duchess!"

"Gammon? Gammon?" said the doctor, while Duchess coughed and choked.

"Don't say that again!" said Ribby, losing her temper—"Here, take this bread and jam, and get out into the yard!"

"Gammon and Spinach! ha ha HA!" shouted Dr. Maggotty triumphantly outside the back door.

"I am feeling very much better my dear Ribby," said Duchess. "Do you not think that I had better go home before it gets dark?"

"Perhaps it might be wise, my dear Duchess. I will lend you a nice warm shawl, and you shall take my arm."

"I would not trouble you for worlds; I feel wonderfully better. One pill of Dr. Maggotty—"

"Indeed it is most admirable, if it has cured you of a patty-pan! I will call directly after breakfast to ask how you have slept."

Ribby and Duchess said goodbye affectionately, and Duchess started home. Half-way up the lane she stopped and looked back; Ribby had gone in and shut her door. Duchess slipped through the fence, and ran round to the back of Ribby's house, and peeped into the yard.

Upon the roof of the pig-stye sat Dr. Maggotty and three jackdaws. The jackdaws were eating pie-crust, and the magpie was drinking gravy out of a patty-pan.

"Gammon, ha, HA!" he shouted when he saw Duchess's little black nose peeping round the corner.

Duchess ran home feeling uncommonly silly!

When Ribby came out for a pailful of water to wash up the tea-things, she found a pink and white pie-dish lying smashed in the middle of the yard. The patty-pan was under the pump, where Dr. Maggotty had considerately left it.

Ribby stared with amazement—"Did you ever see the like! So there really *was* a patty-pan? . . . But *my* patty-pans are all in the kitchen cupboard. Well I never did! . . . Next time I want to give a party—I will invite Cousin Tabitha Twitchit!"

THE END

THE TALE OF
GINGER
AND PICKLES

1909

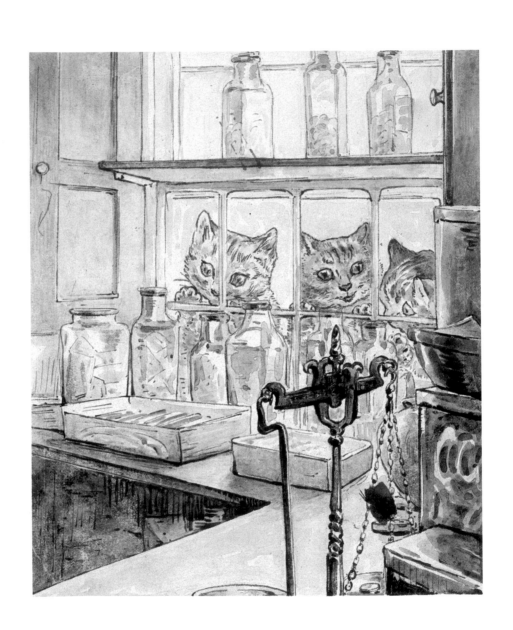

ONCE upon a time there was a village shop. The name over the window was "Ginger and Pickles".

It was a little small shop just the right size for Dolls—Lucinda and Jane Doll-cook always bought their groceries at Ginger and Pickles.

The counter inside was a convenient height for rabbits.

Ginger and Pickles sold red spotty pocket-handkerchiefs at a penny three farthings.

They also sold sugar, and snuff and goloshes.

In fact, although it was such a small shop it sold nearly everything—except a few things that you want in a hurry—like bootlaces, hair-pins and mutton chops.

Ginger and Pickles were the people who kept the shop. Ginger was a yellow tom-cat, and Pickles was a terrier.

The rabbits were always a little bit afraid of Pickles.

The shop was also
patronized by mice—only
the mice were rather
afraid of Ginger.

Ginger usually requested
Pickles to serve them,
because he said it made
his mouth water.

"I cannot bear," said he,
"to see them going out at the
door carrying their little parcels."

"I have the same feeling about rats," replied Pickles, "but it
would never do to eat our own customers; they would leave us
and go to Tabitha Twitchit's."

"On the contrary, they
would go nowhere," replied
Ginger gloomily.

(Tabitha Twitchit kept
the only other shop in the
village. She did not give
credit.)

Ginger and Pickles gave
unlimited credit.

Now the meaning of
"credit" is this—when a
customer buys a bar of soap, instead of the customer pulling out
a purse and paying for it—she says she will pay another time.

And Pickles makes a low bow and says, "With pleasure,
madam," and it is written down in a book.

The customers come again and again, and buy quantities, in
spite of being afraid of Ginger and Pickles.

But there is no money in what is called the "till".

The customers came in crowds every day and bought quantities, especially the toffee customers. But there was always no money; they never paid for as much as a pennyworth of peppermints.

But the sales were enormous, ten times as large as Tabitha Twitchit's.

As there was always no money, Ginger and Pickles were obliged to eat their own goods.

Pickles ate biscuits and Ginger ate a dried haddock.

They ate them by candle-light after the shop was closed.

When it came to Jan. 1st there was still no money, and Pickles was unable to buy a dog licence.

"It is very unpleasant, I am afraid of the police," said Pickles.

"It is your own fault for being a terrier; *I* do not require a licence, and neither does Kep, the Collie dog."

"It is very uncomfortable, I am afraid I shall be summoned. I have tried in vain to get a licence upon credit at the Post Office;" said Pickles. "The place is full of policemen. I met one as I was coming home."

"Let us send in the bill again to Samuel Whiskers, Ginger, he owes 22/9 for bacon."

"I do not believe that he intends to pay at all," replied Ginger.

"And I feel sure that Anna Maria pockets things—Where are all the cream crackers?"

"You have eaten them yourself," replied Ginger.

Ginger and Pickles retired into the back parlour. They did accounts. They added up sums and sums, and sums.

"Samuel Whiskers has run up a bill as long as his tail; he has had an ounce and three-quarters of snuff since October."

"What is seven pounds of butter at 1/3, and a stick of sealing wax and four matches?"

"Send in all the bills again to everybody 'with comp^ts'," replied Ginger.

After a time they heard a noise in the shop, as if something had been pushed in at the door. They came out of the back parlour. There was an envelope lying on the counter, and a policeman writing in a notebook!

Pickles nearly had a fit, he barked and he barked and made little rushes.

"Bite him, Pickles! bite him!" spluttered Ginger behind a sugar-barrel, "he's only a German doll!"

The policeman went on writing in his note-book; twice he put his pencil in his mouth, and once he dipped it in the treacle.

Pickles barked till he was hoarse. But still the policeman took no notice. He had bead eyes, and his helmet was sewed on with stitches.

At length on his last little rush—Pickles found that the shop was empty. The policeman had disappeared.

But the envelope remained. "Do you think that he has gone to fetch a real live policeman? I am afraid it is a summons," said Pickles.

"No," replied Ginger, who had opened the envelope, "it is the rates and taxes, £3 19 11¾."

"This is the last straw," said Pickles, "let us close the shop."

They put up the shutters, and left. But they have not removed from the neighbourhood. In fact some people wish they had gone further.

Ginger is living in the warren. I do not know what occupation he pursues; he looks stout and comfortable.

Pickles is at present a gamekeeper.

The closing of the shop caused great inconvenience. Tabitha Twitchit immediately raised the price of everything a half-penny; and she continued to refuse to give credit.

Of course there are the tradesmen's carts—
the butcher, the fish-man
and Timothy Baker.

But a person cannot live
on "seed wigs" and sponge-
cake and butter-buns—not
even when the sponge-cake
is as good as Timothy's!

After a time Mr. John Dormouse and his daughter began to
sell peppermints and candles.

But they did not keep "self-fitting sixes"; and it takes five
mice to carry one seven inch candle.